The PaiN and the Great One
Friend or fiend?

The Pain and the Great One
Friend or fiend?

Judy Blume

Illustrated by
Kate Pankhurst

MACMILLAN CHILDREN'S BOOKS

To Emma and Ben Valentine, my Tashmoo Friends

First published 2008 by Delacorte Press, an imprint of
Random House Children's Books, New York

This edition published 2008 by Macmillan Children's Books
a division of Macmillan Publishers Limited
20 New Wharf Road, London N1 9RR
Basingstoke and Oxford
Associated companies throughout the world
www.panmacmillan.com

ISBN 978-0-230-70029-1

A CIP catalogue record for this book is available from
the British Library.

Printed and bound in the UK by CPI Mackays, Chatham ME5 8TD

Contents

Meet the Pain

My sister's name is Abigail. I call her *The Great One* because she thinks she's so great. She says, "I don't think it, I know it!" When she says that I laugh like crazy. Then she gets mad. It's fun to make her mad. Who cares if she's in third grade and I'm just in first? That doesn't make her faster. Or stronger. Or even smarter. I don't get why Mom and Dad act like she's so special. Sometimes I think they love her more than me.

Meet the Great One

My brother's name is Jacob but everyone calls him Jake. Everyone but me. I call him *The Pain* because that's what he is. He's a first-grade pain. And he will always be a pain — even if he lives to be a hundred. Even then, I'll be two years older than him. I'll still know more about everything. And I'll always know exactly what he's thinking. That's just the way it is. I don't get why Mom and Dad act like he's so special. Sometimes I think they love him more than me.

Ben Is My Fiend

The Pain

Today at school my teacher, Mary, called my group to the reading circle. Everyone else read at their tables or in the book corner. Mary said, "Justin, will you start?" When we go to the reading circle we read from a special book called *People and Pets*. Justin read a story about a dog named Goldie.

Then Lila read about a cat called Sammy. Sammy the cat wasn't anything

like my cat. "I could write a better story about Fluzzy," I told Mary.

Mary said, "I'd like to see that story, Jake." Then she asked me to read. Just as I was about to start, another teacher came into our room and whispered something to

 6

Mary. "I have to step into the hall for a minute," Mary told our group. "I'll be right back." She looked at me. "Go ahead, Jake."

"The name of this story is 'Ben'," I said. I cleared my throat twice. "*Ben is my fiend*." Maggie laughed. I didn't know why. So I kept reading. "*I'm glad he's my fiend because . . .*"

Everyone but David laughed this time. Justin laughed so hard he fell off his chair. When he did, his chair toppled over too. That made everyone laugh harder.

"What?" I said to my group.

"*Fiend?*" Maggie said. "Ben is your *fiend?*"

My group couldn't stop laughing. Even David laughed.

Wendy, our helper teacher, came across the room. She sat in Mary's chair. "What's up?" she asked.

"He thinks . . ." Maggie started to say.

"He thinks . . ." But she was laughing so hard she couldn't finish.

So Lila finished for her. "He thinks Ben is his *fiend*."

"What's a fiend?" David asked.

I was wondering the same thing.

"Justin, pick up your chair," Wendy said. Then she looked at me. "Jake, do you know what a fiend is?"

"No," I said.

"Can anyone help us?" Wendy asked.

Justin didn't raise his hand. He just spit it out. "A fiend is a monster! A fiend is evil."

I felt my face turn hot. I felt really stupid.

"Jake," Wendy said, "look at the picture of the two boys in the story."

The boys in the picture were laughing. They looked like friends. "Now . . . why don't you start reading again," Wendy said.

"*Ben is my fiend*," I began. I meant to say

friend. But *fiend* just slipped out.

Now my group was out of control.

"Let's settle down, please," Wendy said. She printed both words on the board. "Jake, can you find the difference between *friend* and *fiend*?"

I looked at both words. They looked almost the same. But one had an *r* and one didn't. So I said, "Oh, I get it! A *fiend* is a *friend* without the *r*."

Now my group went crazy. Wendy couldn't get them to stop. I wanted to disappear. I pictured myself walking out of class, down the hall, out the front door and all the way home. Instead I just sat there. When Maggie laughs it sounds like she's screaming. When David laughs he sounds like a seal. Justin holds his breath when he laughs. His face gets so red it looks like he's about to explode.

 9

The rest of the class was wondering what was going on. You could hear them whispering.

Wendy clapped her hands. "OK, that's enough! Maggie, take a turn reading, please."

"Where should I start?" Maggie asked when she finally calmed down.

"Why don't you start at the beginning of the story," Wendy said.

Maggie took a big breath. Then she started to read. "*Ben is my* fiend. *I'm glad he's my* fiend *because . . .*"

But no one was listening. They were shrieking and stomping their feet. Lila held her stomach. "It hurts . . ." she cried. "It hurts to laugh so hard!"

Wendy said, "Maggie . . . the word is *friend*!" You could tell from her voice that she'd had enough.

"I know!" Maggie said.

"Then why did you say *fiend*?" Wendy asked.

"I didn't mean to . . ."

That's when Mary came back into the room. "Everything OK?" she asked Wendy, looking at us. Mary always knows when something is going on.

"Just a little mix-up," Wendy explained, giving Mary back her chair.

Later, in the playground, my class made a circle like when we were in kindergarten. But instead of "Duck, duck, goose", Lila called, "Friend, friend, fiend!" She tapped *me* for *fiend*. I had to run around the circle trying to catch her. It didn't feel good. It didn't feel funny. Then everyone did it. Even Justin. And he's supposed to be my best friend. That was the worst.

★

At dinner the Great One looked at me and
said, "What's wrong?"

"Who says anything's wrong?"

"I can tell."

Mom said, "Is something wrong, Jake?"

"I made a mistake in reading group." I
pushed my pasta around on my plate.

"Everyone makes mistakes," Mom said.

"Not *this* mistake."

"I'm sure it wasn't that bad," Dad said.

"Oh yes, it was!" I told him.

Mom, Dad and the Great One waited for me to tell them more. But I didn't. The Great One started guessing. "Did you say a bad word? Is that it?"

"No."

"Did you leave out a word?"

"No."

"Did you mix up two words?"

"Maybe," I said. How did she know that was it?

"Everyone does that," she said. "It's no big deal."

But it was a big deal to me.

The next day at school when Maggie saw me she said, "Hi, *fiend*!" Everyone laughed.

In the playground I didn't play any games. I climbed to the top of the monkey bars and stayed there. "Help . . . *fiend!*" Victor called, pointing to me. Everyone laughed again.

The next day at morning meeting, Mary asked if I could give the weather report. I shook my head, even though I knew the weather. So Justin got to be weather reporter instead. And Dylan got to ask the riddle of the day. "When is it dangerous to play cards?"

I knew the answer, but I wouldn't raise my hand. I was never raising my hand again. So Mary called on Marco. He said,

"When the joker is wild."

Everyone clapped for Dylan's riddle and Marco's answer.

Later, Mary sat next to me during reading time. She said, "What are you reading, Jake?"

I showed her the book. *Reptiles Around the World*.

"You want to read just to me?" she asked.

I shook my head.

"You want to keep reading to yourself?"

I nodded.

"OK," Mary said.

I didn't tell her I was never reading out loud again.

On the school bus going home I sat next to Justin. But I didn't talk. I faced away from him and looked out the window. So Justin joked around with Dylan, who sat behind him. When we got off the bus Justin said, "Guess what I'm going to be for Halloween?"

"What?" I said.

"A *fiend*! Isn't that the best idea?"

I didn't answer. I ran the rest of the way home. I could hear Justin calling, "Jake – wait for me! Jake –" But I didn't wait.

At home I got a big piece of paper and wrote: Justin is a fiend.

That night, when Mom finished reading to me, I said, "Justin's going to be a *fiend* for Halloween."

"What are you going to be?" she asked.

"Nothing. I'm not going trick-or-treating."

Mom looked at me. "OK, but if you change your mind, I'll help with your costume."

"I'm not wearing a costume."

Mom kissed me goodnight. When she was gone, I got out of bed and tiptoed to my closet. I reached up and grabbed my Wolfman mask. Grandma bought it for me over the summer. It's pretty scary. I pulled it on. "What do you think, Fluzzy? Do I look like a fiend?" Fluzzy yawned. What does he care about fiends? Then I yanked off the mask and got back into bed. Bruno was waiting for me. *Bruno* is my best friend now.

On Halloween night the Great One danced into the living room. She was wearing a tutu, cowboy boots and a red wig. She carried a magnifying glass. "How do you like it?" she asked. "What are you supposed to be?" "You can't tell?" I didn't answer. She sighed. "I guess you're just not old enough to know." "Know what?" "Spy Dancer."

"Who's Spy Dancer?"

"Never mind!" She turned and twirled to the front door. She was going trick-or-treating with her friends.

"We could go trick-or-treating too," Dad said to me.

"I'm not going trick-or-treating." I put on my Wolfman mask, and every time the bell rang I opened the door. A couple of little kids screamed when they saw me. One girl said, "What are you supposed to be?"

"A fiend," I told her.

"What's a fiend?"

"It's the opposite of a friend."

"Oh," she said, reaching into the candy bowl. She helped herself to three mini-boxes of raisins. At least I think that's what they were. It's not that easy to see when you're wearing a Wolfman mask.

The next time the bell rang it was

19

Justin. I saw his dad waiting for him on the sidewalk. He was wearing a monster mask, but I recognized him anyway. Last year we went trick-or-treating together.

"Are you supposed to be what I think you're supposed to be?" he asked.

"Yes," I told him. And I growled. He growled too and took a handful of candy from the bowl. Then we just stood there looking at each other through the eyeholes in our monster masks. Finally Justin said, "I have an idea."

I said, "Me too."

"You go first," Justin said.

"No, you go first."

"OK," Justin said. "Remember last year when we went trick-or-treating together?"
I nodded.
"We could do that again."
I pretended to think it over.
Then I said, "Deal."

I found Dad and told him I'd changed my mind. I was going trick-or-treating after all. Dad helped me into my jacket and gave me a loot bag.

"Ready?" Justin asked when I came back.

"Ready," I said.

We jumped off the porch and ran down the street together.

Later, when I got home, I ate two Crunch bars from my loot bag. Then I added an *r* to the sign that said *Justin is a fiend!*

Useless

The Great One

We're going to Uncle Phil's apartment in New York. You have to drive through a tunnel to get there. Either that or drive over a bridge. But the tunnel is faster for us. The Pain doesn't like tunnels. "Tell me when . . ." he kept saying to Mom.

As we came up to the entrance of the tunnel Mom said, "OK . . . now."

And the Pain slid to the floor of the back seat of our car. He covered his eyes

with his hands.
"Tell me when
we're out."
"You are beyond
hopeless," I told him.
"Abigail . . ."
Mom warned.
"It's just a road,"
I argued.

"An underwater road," the Pain said
from the floor.

"And he's not in his seat belt," I added.

"Thank you, Abigail," Mom said.

"Thank you for what?" I asked.

I could hear Mom sigh.

"You'd better not get carsick while you're
down there," I said to the Pain.

"I'm not carsick," the Pain said.

"Because puking in the car isn't allowed,"
I told him.

"Abigail . . ." Mom said. "Stop talking about it or you'll make him sick."

"Me? Make him carsick? Why would I want to do that?"

"That's enough, Abigail," Mom said.

As we came out of the tunnel Mom called to the Pain, "All clear!" And the Pain sat in his seat again and fastened his seat belt.

"Invisible line," I reminded him. *Invisible line* is how we divide the back seat of the car. I have my side and he has his. But he gave me a kick anyway.

So I gave him one back.

"Children," Mom said, "Dad can't concentrate on the road when you're acting up."

We got to Uncle Phil's apartment in time for lunch. But there was no sign of food. Our cousins William and Sierra were there.

William is twelve and Sierra is fifteen. Last time we saw them was before Uncle Phil got divorced and moved to New York. When Mom asked if she could help get lunch ready, Uncle Phil looked surprised. He tore off the top of a paper bag and scribbled a shopping list on it. Then he gave Sierra some money and told her and William to go to the big deli on the corner. William pointed at the Pain and me. "What are *they* . . . useless?" Before I could say anything, before I could

tell him *Useless is as useless does* or something
like that, Sierra laughed. "Yeah," she said.
"They can help us carry everything home."

I didn't want to go anywhere with
William and Sierra.

"Jake and Abigail don't know their way
around New York," Mom said.

"You think *we* do?" Sierra said. "This is
the first time we're visiting our dad since he
moved here."

"Why don't I come with you?" Mom
said.

"If *you're* going, you don't need William
and me," Sierra said to Mom. "Besides, I
have a lot to do."

"Like what?" William asked.

"None of your business," Sierra told him.

"*None of your business,*" William sang,
mocking his sister.

Sierra looked like she wanted to slug him.

The Pain looked at me. I knew what he was thinking – William and Sierra are worse than us. Much worse.

"You kids are going," Uncle Phil told William and Sierra, "and that's that!"

"Fine," Sierra said. And she grabbed the list out of Uncle Phil's hand.

Mom said, "Abigail and Jake will come with us. That will give Uncle Phil and Dad some time alone."

Why would Dad want to be alone with Uncle Phil? I wondered. Uncle Phil isn't a fun uncle. He's nothing like Uncle Mitch. Mitch taught me to ride my bike. I don't think Uncle Phil likes kids. I'm not sure he likes anyone, not even William and Sierra. He and Dad are complete opposites. I don't see how they can be brothers.

★

The deli was huge. It took up a whole block. It was busy too. There were lines everywhere. Mom took charge. "William, get on the bread line."

"Do I have to?"

"Yes," Mom said, "if you ever want to have lunch." Then she told Sierra to get a number and wait on line at the deli meats counter.

"No way," Sierra said. "I'm a veggie. I don't go near that stuff."

"OK . . ." Mom said. "You can pick up the cheese and the rest of what's on the list. I'll wait on line here."

"*She* has to help me," Sierra said, pointing at me.

"My name is Abigail," I told her.

"Whatever," Sierra said.

Sierra used to be nice. One time when I was little we baked cupcakes together.

I followed her through the deli. "I hate this city," she said, loud enough for anyone to hear. A couple of people turned to look at her. "You can't ride your horse or anything."

"You have a horse?" I asked.

Sierra said, "We have six horses. You probably don't know, but we moved to Montana with our mom. You probably don't even know where Montana is."

"Yes, I do," I told her. I tried to picture the map of the states on the wall in my classroom. Montana . . . Montana . . . which state was Montana?

"It's out west," Sierra told me.

"I know that," I said.

"I ride my horse to school."

"That sounds so cool."

"You know what's not cool?" she asked.

"What?"

"You and your family. And that includes my dad."

"That's rude," I told her.

She laughed and shoved the list in my face. "Get this stuff. I've got to text my boyfriend." She pushed a basket at me, then took off.

I didn't know what to get. I mean, I could read the list, but there were about fifty kinds of mustard on the shelf. I threw in the one with the fanciest label. Next on the list was olive oil. There were rows and rows of olive oil. I chose the one in the prettiest bottle. But what kind of cheese was I supposed to get? I stood in front of the cheese counter. There were so many! A hundred, at least. I didn't recognize any of the names.

"Do you need some help?" a woman asked.

"I need cheese," I told her.

"What kind?"

"I don't know. For lunch."

"How about Cheddar?" she said.

"Is it white? My brother only eats white food."

She reached for a chunk of cheese and handed it to me. "I think this will do the trick," she said.

I thanked her, then looked around for Sierra. I didn't see her anywhere, so I ran through the store looking for Mom. I kept going down the wrong aisles. Once I passed William. "Hey," he called. "Cousin . . ." Like he couldn't remember my name.

Finally I found Mom and the Pain. Mom was still waiting for her number to be called. "Where's Sierra?" she asked.

I shrugged.

"Why didn't you stay with her?"

I shrugged again.

Mom took my basket. "I didn't know which kind of mustard to get . . . or olive oil . . . or cheese . . ."

"You did a good job," Mom said.

"Did you get something for me?" the Pain asked.

"White cheese," I told him.

He nodded. "Good."

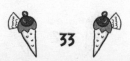

33

When all our shopping was done Mom found Sierra outside the store, yakking on her cellphone. Mom handed each of us a bag to carry, and she carried two.

We were almost back at Uncle Phil's when I tripped on the kerb and fell. The bag I was carrying flew out of my hand. Lemons rolled down the sidewalk, packages of deli meat flew out and a bag of sandwich rolls landed with a thud.

"Oh, honey . . ." Mom said, helping me up. "Are you OK?"

I looked down at my knees. They were scraped and bloody and one of them had pebbles stuck to it. I definitely wasn't OK.

"Jake," Mom called, "get those lemons! William, pick up the rolls and the deli meats."

Sierra shook her head. "Useless . . ." she said, looking at my knees.

"Really, Sierra . . ." Mom said. "Surely you can be kinder than that."

"I don't think so," Sierra muttered.

Mom handed Sierra money and asked her to go to the closest pharmacy. "We need antiseptic and Band-Aids," Mom told her. "Unless your dad has them at the apartment."

"How would I know?" Sierra said.

"Let's not take a chance," Mom said. "Just go and get them. There's a pharmacy on almost every block. Then come back to the apartment."

"You expect a lot," Sierra told Mom.

Mom muttered something to herself.

While the Pain chased lemons, William opened the package of sandwich rolls and shoved one in his mouth.

"William . . ." Mom said.

"I'm hungry," William told her.

"We're all hungry," Mom said.

"And some of us are injured," I added, in case he didn't know. Blood trickled down one of my legs, and my knees burned like crazy.

When we got back to the apartment, Dad met us at the door. Mom shoved the shopping bags at him and said, "Don't ask . . ." Then she took me to the bathroom and washed my knees.

"Ouch . . ." I kept saying. But when Sierra got back with the alcohol they burned even worse. Mom kept saying she was sorry but she had to make sure they were clean.

At last we sat down to lunch. Dad was the only one still in a good mood. He tried to get Sierra and William to talk. He asked them questions about school. They didn't answer. He tried riddles, but only the Pain laughed at the answers.

Then he tried to get Uncle Phil to talk about when they were growing up. That was a big mistake.

"Let me tell you what it was like back then," Uncle Phil said to the rest of us, and I didn't like the way he smiled. "Little Andy could do no wrong." Andy is Dad's name. "Little Andy was everyone's favourite. Just ask him."

"Come on, Phil. . . ." Dad said. "We're grown-ups now . . . it's time to let that go."

But Sierra jumped in. "I know just how you feel, Dad," she said, "because William is the favourite in *our* family and I'm less than zero. Isn't that right?"

"I like being the favourite," William said.

"I'm sure I'd like being the favourite too," Sierra said.

The Pain looked over at me.

"What are you kids talking about?" Uncle Phil finally asked. "I don't play favourites."

It got really quiet. So I said, "Did you know Sierra rides her horse to school in Montana? Isn't that cool?"

William snorted. He sounded like a horse.

"Montana?" Uncle Phil said. Then his voice boomed. "Her horse?"

"She has six horses." I knew I should stop, but I couldn't help myself.

"Six horses?" Uncle Phil repeated.

Sierra shouted, "Yes, six horses! That's how it could be if you and Mom—"

Uncle Phil didn't wait for her to finish. "That's enough, Sierra!" Sierra's face turned red. She shoved back her chair and ran for the bathroom. The door slammed.

"This is a fun lunch," William said.

That's when the Pain spilled his milk all

over William. "Useless!" William shouted at him. "Look at this . . . I'm soaked."

Mom jumped up to get kitchen towels. I could tell the Pain wanted to cry. He got out of his seat, went over to Dad and rested his head against Dad's shoulder. "Can we go now?" he whispered.

"Soon," Dad said. Then he looked at Uncle Phil. "Phil, I think—"

"I don't give a hooey what you think, Andy! So keep it to yourself for once."

We left Uncle Phil's right after lunch. Dad was really upset. Usually nothing bothers him, but this time was different. "My brother and those kids . . ." he said so quietly I could hardly hear him.

"They're teenagers," Mom reminded him. "They're going through a lot."

"Don't worry, Dad," I said. "We're never

40

going to be like William and Sierra. Right, Jake?"

"They're *fiends*," the Pain said.

"They behaved badly," Mom said. "I won't argue with that."

"They called us *useless*!" I said.

"The divorce has been hard on them," Mom said.

"They have their own horses," I said.

Mom and Dad looked at each other. "Sierra probably wishes they had horses," Mom said.

"You mean she doesn't have her own horse?"

Dad shook his head.

"But how do you know? They live in Montana."

Mom and Dad looked at each other again. "Actually they live in Cincinnati," Mom said.

"Is that in Montana?" I asked.

"No, it's a city in Ohio," Dad said.

"You mean Sierra was lying?" I asked.

"Sometimes there's a fine line between lying and wishing," Mom said.

"That's just a nice way to say she was lying," I said. And then I remembered the time I told my friends I could ride a bike when I couldn't. Did that mean I was like Sierra?

"Where's Ohio?" the Pain asked.

"When we get home I'll show you on a map," Dad said.

Mom looked around. "It's such a beautiful day. It's a shame to waste it. How about a quick trip to the zoo in Central Park?"

Mom always comes up with good ideas. So we went to the zoo and watched the penguins. And all the way home the Pain

and I were really nice to each other, even going through the tunnel.

When we got home Dad spread out the atlas on the floor. An atlas is a big book of maps. Dad's is very old. He got it when he graduated from high school. He showed us Cincinnati on the map of Ohio.

The Pain said, "I'm glad Sierra's not my sister." And I said, "I'm glad William's not my brother." Then we both jumped on Dad.

"And we're really, really glad Uncle Phil's not our dad."

Dad hugged us and said, "And I'm really glad you two are my kids."

She Stole My Story

The Great One

I told Sasha about Sunday at Uncle Phil's.
I told her how William and Sierra called
us *useless*. Then I made her promise never to
tell anyone, not even Emily or Kaylee.

That afternoon our teacher, Mr Gee,
said, "Today we're going to write a story in
class."

"Is it a *never take your pencil off the paper*
story?" Lucas asked.

"Yes," Mr Gee said. "From the time I

say *go* to the time I
say *stop,* just write,
write, write."
"About what?"
Emily asked.
"Something
that happened to
you," Mr Gee said. "This time let's make it
about something you didn't like."

When Mr Gee said, "Go!" I started
writing. I wrote about the time we visited
a farm and a goose chased me. He honked

and snapped at my behind. I screamed until Dad rescued me.

I kept writing, writing, writing until Mr Gee called, "Pencils down!" Then he asked who would like to read their story to the class. Half the class raised their hands, including me. Mr Gee called on Sasha.

Sasha went to the front of the room. "The name of my story is 'Useless', " she said.

I looked up.

Then she started to read. And the story she started to read was *my* story — the story I'd told her about visiting Uncle Phil. Only she wrote it like it happened to *her* instead of to me. I couldn't believe it. I trusted her when she promised she'd never ever tell, and now she was telling the whole world. My heart started beating really fast. I felt like grabbing her paper and ripping it to shreds.

When she finished Mr Gee said, "Good work, Sasha."

Sasha smiled.

As soon as I could, I went over to her desk. "You stole my story!"

"Not really," she said. "I just wrote about it."

"But it happened to me, not you!"

"So?"

"So, we're supposed to be friends. And friends don't steal from each other."

"I didn't think you'd mind," Sasha said. "I thought you'd like the idea."

"You what?"

"You heard me, Abigail," she said. "I thought you'd like the idea."

"Liar!" I shouted. Our class got very

49

quiet. Everyone was listening. But I didn't care.

"You have no right to call me names," Sasha said very quietly.

"I'm never speaking to you again," I told her.

"Fine, then I'm never speaking to you either."

"I said it first," I told her.

"I *thought* it first," she said.

"You copy everything," I told her. "Even my thoughts!"

"Copying is the highest form of flattery," she said.

"Who told you that?" I asked.

"My mother," she said.

"Then maybe your mother is a copycat too. Maybe your mother steals from her friends, just like you!"

"Abigail!" Mr Gee said sharply. "Sasha!"

I went up to Mr Gee. But before I could say *She stole my story,* the bell rang and the school day was over.

I didn't sit near Sasha on the bus going home. I sat with Emily. I told her the whole story. "No wonder you're mad," she said.

That night, before dinner, Mom asked if I was feeling OK. "I hate Sasha!" I said.

"But Sasha's your friend," Mom said.

"*Was* my friend."

Mom took the chicken out of the oven. "Want to talk about it?"

So while she was dishing out the green beans and potatoes I told her how Sasha stole my story.

"That must have hurt," Mom said.

"It did. It hurt really bad."

Telling Mom made me feel better. So at

dinner I told Dad how Sasha stole my story. "She wrote it exactly the way I told it to her."

"Did she write about me?" the Pain asked.

"Not every story is about you," I said.

Then I went on and on. "She even wrote about my knees." I stopped for a minute, to check them. They didn't have scabs yet.

"I wanted to rip the paper out of her hand and tear it into teeny tiny bits."

"You should have," the Pain said. Before we went to bed the Pain asked, "How do you spell *Sasha*?"

I spelled it out for him. A few minutes later he brought a sign to my room. It said: *Sasha is a Fiend!* He helped me tape it to the wall above my bed. "Thank you," I said.

The Pain smiled.

The next morning on the school bus I didn't look at Sasha. She didn't look at me either. It was the same in class. And in the playground.

That afternoon Mr Gee called us up to his desk. Before he even asked what was going on, I blurted it out. "That story Sasha read yesterday . . . she stole it from me."

"My mother says copying is the highest form of flattery," Sasha repeated.

Mr Gee looked at Sasha, then he looked at me. "I hope you two can work this out on your own," he said.

Madison Purdy got all the girls in our class to choose sides. She made it me against Sasha. I can't stand Madison Purdy. One time at ballet she called me a weed. Now she acted like she was in charge of the whole world. Emily sided with me. Kaylee sided with Sasha. My stomach hurt almost all the time.

On Friday Mr Gee called Sasha and me up to his desk again. "This has gone far enough."

"But . . ." I started to say.

"No *buts*," Mr Gee said.

"*If only* Madison . . ." Sasha began, but Mr Gee stopped her, too.

"No *if onlys*."

"Give us one more chance," Sasha said.

"OK," Mr Gee said. "But this is it."

In the playground my group huddled to one side and Sasha's group huddled to the other. Everybody had ideas of what we should do. But we couldn't agree on anything. Finally Sasha and Kaylee came over to us. The other girls backed away until it was just me and Emily and Kaylee and Sasha. Kaylee said, "Sasha has something to say to you, Abigail." She gave Sasha a little nudge.

"I'm sorry I used your story," Sasha said.

"You mean *stole* my story," I said.

"She didn't steal it," Kaylee said. "She borrowed it."

Emily said, "You can't borrow something if you don't ask first."

"I never thought of that," Kaylee said. She looked at Sasha. "Emily's right. It's like you can't borrow my jacket unless you ask and then I say OK."

Sasha was quiet for a minute. "From now on I'll ask," she said.

"And when a friend tells you something that's private you won't blab it all over town?" I said.

"I didn't blab it," Sasha said. "Nobody knew it was your family until *you* blabbed it."

That was probably true, I thought. But still . . .

Mr Gee came over to us. "How's it going?"

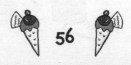

Now Kaylee and Emily backed away, leaving just me and Sasha. "You want to know why I did it?" Sasha asked. "Because my family is so boring. Nothing ever happens in my family."

"Sasha," Mr Gee said, "can you understand why Abigail feels you betrayed her?"

"I guess." Sasha choked up. "But *she* dissed my mom. She said my mom steals from her friends."

"I said *maybe* your mom steals from her friends."

Mr Gee rocked back and forth on his heels.

I knew what I had to do. I just didn't want to do it. "OK," I said, and I took a big breath. "I'm sorry I dissed your mom."

"You're really sorry?" Sasha said.

"Yes."

"Good."

"Well," Mr Gee said, "I'm glad you two worked out your problems." He went over to a group of boys.

Sasha turned to me and said, "I'll tell you a secret if you promise not to tell."

"I promise."

"This was the worst week of my life. I couldn't even eat, my stomach hurt so bad."

I didn't tell her how bad *my* stomach hurt. Instead I told her about the sign over my bed, the one that says *Sasha is a fiend!* "But I'm going to take it down today."

"You really thought I was a *fiend*?"

"Actually my brother made the sign and gave it to me."

"Your brother thought I was a *fiend*?"

"Well, yes . . . because you stole my story."

"I don't see how I can be friends with someone who thought I was a fiend."

"I *said* it was my brother, not me."

"But you put the sign over your bed!"

I never should have told her about the sign. What was I thinking?

Emily and Kaylee came up to us. "So, you two are friends again, right?" Emily asked.

Sasha and I looked at each other. "Friends or fiends," Sasha said. "We haven't decided yet."

"It's better to be friends," Emily and Kaylee said at the same time. They slapped hands, spun around three times and pretended to spit.

Sasha and I started laughing. We laughed all the way back to our classroom.

Snow Day

The Pain

"**S**now day!" I jumped on to the Great One's bed. "School's closed." I shook her. "Come on, wake up!"

"Mmmph . . . bafa . . ." she mumbled.

I shook her again. "Open your eyes."

She swatted at me like I was a mosquito. I grabbed her feet and started pulling. I pulled her right off the bed. She landed on the rug with a thud. But she still didn't open her eyes. So I dragged her across the floor to

the window. This time she opened her eyes.
"Look!" I said, pointing at the window.
"This better be good." She knelt in front

of the window and looked outside. "Snow?" she said.

"That's what I've been trying to tell you."

The Great One climbed back into bed and pulled the quilt over her head.

Why wasn't she excited?

I looked into Mom and Dad's room, but they were still sleeping.

"Why isn't anyone else excited?" I asked Fluzzy. He just looked at me.

I crept downstairs to the kitchen. Fluzzy flew by me. He waited at the bottom of the stairs and miaowed. I knew what that meant. I got out the box of cat food and carried it to his dish. But before I could fill it I had to take out the three toy mice he'd stashed there. Every night, while we're sleeping, Fluzzy plays with his toy mice. We don't know why he leaves them in his food dish. I lifted them out by their tails. Fluzzy watched as I sniffed them. They smelled like the inside of his mouth.

The Great One won't touch Fluzzy's mice. She says they're disgusting. Probably that's why Fluzzy likes me best. The Great One can't stand that Fluzzy sleeps on my bed. It makes her crazy that I'm Fluzzy's favourite. Maybe if she'd sniff his mice he'd like her better. I gave Fluzzy fresh water and poured food into his bowl.

While he chowed down
I opened the front door
and stuck out my head.
Brrrr . . . it was freezing. But I
didn't care how cold it was. I pulled
my snow jacket over my pyjamas, got
into my snow boots and grabbed a hat
and mittens. I closed the door behind
me so Fluzzy couldn't get out.

I almost slid down the front steps
because the snow was so deep
you couldn't tell exactly where
they were. Everything was white.
I jumped off the steps. The snow
was fluffy. It wasn't as high as
my waist, but it came up past my
knees.

I clomped around the front yard. I started
trying to build a fort, but it wasn't that
much fun by myself. So I gave up and rolled

in the snow. I rolled all the way across our front yard. And all the way back.

By then I had snow down my neck. My pyjama bottoms were soaked. Plus I was hungry. So I went to the front door. But the doorknob wouldn't turn. I banged on it. I rang the bell ten times. I called, "Hello . . . let me in!"

Fluzzy came to the window next to the

door and looked out at me. "Go get Mom or Dad," I told him. He pawed at the glass, but that was all. I banged again. Louder this time. "Hello . . . somebody . . . anybody . . ."

Finally the Great One opened the door. She looked me up and down.

"Why are you wearing pyjamas in the snow?"

I didn't answer.

"You'd better change before Mom sees you."

But it was too late. Mom was already coming down the stairs. "Jake . . . you went out in the snow in your pyjamas?" she said, like she couldn't believe it. "What were you thinking?"

I wasn't thinking anything except about the snow, but I didn't tell that to Mom.

"Go upstairs and change into dry

clothes," Mom said. "And bring me those wet pyjamas."

Fluzzy smiled. Some people think cats can't smile, but I know they can. Sometimes Fluzzy laughs, even if I'm the only one who knows it.

★

We were just about finished with breakfast when Justin came to the door. "Can Jake come out to play?" he asked Dad.

"Snow fort!" we yelled when we were outside. We started building in the front yard. Dylan came over. Then a couple of other boys. Then Michael and Eric from fifth grade. We all worked together. I wished every day could be a snow day!

When the Great One's friends came over she raced out of the house with Fluzzy right behind her.

Eric shouted, "No girls allowed in our fort!"

"Who'd want to be in your fort?" the Great One said. She and her friends laughed and went to the backyard.

Fluzzy sniffed the air. He tasted the snow. Then very slowly, he tried walking in it. I

called to him, "Come on, Fluzz . . . you can do it."

That's when Madison Purdy and her little brother, Brett, showed up. What were they doing at our house? The Great One says if Madison Purdy was the last person on earth, she still wouldn't be friends with her.

Fluzzy flew over the snow to our fort. Madison Purdy stopped in her tracks when she saw him. "I know that cat."

"No, you don't," I said.

"He looks just like my cat who ran away."

"Well, he's not," I told her. "He's *my* cat."

"No, really . . ." she said. "I think it *is* Mister."

"It's not Mister," I argued. "It's Fluzzy." I wondered who would name a cat *Mister*?

"I don't care if you stole my cat," she

said. "Because Mister was stupid and mean. He was always hissing."

Fluzzy took one look at Madison Purdy, hissed and ran for his life. He ducked under the porch of our house.

Madison watched. "Didn't that cat look like Mister?" she asked Brett.

"Mister was a bad cat," Brett said. "He didn't like me."

"That's because you pulled his tail."

"I pulled his tail because he didn't like me."

"Just stay away from *my* cat," I told them both.

"Where are the girls?" Madison asked. "I heard they were over here."

"In the back," I told her.

Madison headed for the backyard, dragging Brett with her.

I went back to work on our fort with the other boys. It was a big fort. The biggest snow fort ever. But before we'd finished building it, before we'd even started making snowballs, someone yelled, "*Attack!*" and the girls came rushing at us, pounding us with snowballs.

Thwack!

Smash!

Oomph!

Ouch!

We fought back. We scooped together snowballs as fast as we could, but by then the girls were leaping over our fort, jumping on to our backs. Justin went down. Dylan went down. *Wham!* I was tackled from behind and pushed face down in the snow. I tried to yell for help. I tried to kick. But someone sat on my legs and held my head down. I couldn't breathe. Just when I thought that might be the end of me, someone else pulled her off.

"What do you think you're doing to my brother?" It was the Great One.

"Washing his face in snow," Madison Purdy said.

"How would you feel if I washed *your* little brother's face in snow?" the Great One asked Madison.

"I wouldn't mind," Madison said. "He deserves it."

"So do you!" The Great One scooped up a handful of snow and shoved it in Madison's face.

Brett jumped up and down, clapping his hands. "Do it again!"

Madison said, "Shut up, Brett!" She

grabbed his arm and pulled him away.
"Let's get out of here."

"And don't come back!" the Great One
shouted. "That means never!"

"Never would be too soon for me!"
Madison yelled.

As they were leaving Michael yelled,
"Truce!" And the
snowballs stopped
flying.

Then Eric
shouted,
"Sledding
on Holden
Hill!"

In two minutes all the kids were racing home to get their sleds.

The Great One ran for the garage to get hers. "This is the best day in the history of the world!" she sang. "You were right to be excited. Maybe it'll snow again tonight. Maybe tomorrow will be another snow day."

But I was thinking, One snow day at a time is enough for me. Fluzzy came out from under the house. I'm pretty sure he was thinking the same thing.

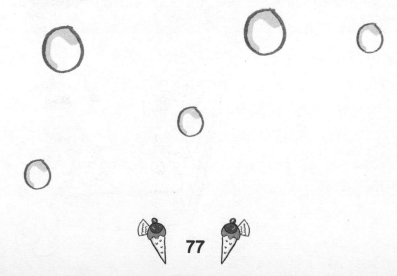

How Fluzzy Got His Name

The Pain

I like thunder, but Fluzzy doesn't. After supper tonight we had a thunderstorm. When Fluzzy heard the first rumble he flew up the stairs. I knew where he was going — to his favourite hiding place: the bathroom closet, way in back, on top of the towels.

Charlie was babysitting the Great One and me. The three of us were playing Uno at the kitchen table. Lightning lit up the sky.

Then *crash!* "That was a big one!" I shouted. I had to shout because the Great One had cotton wool stuffed in her ears. She says she's not afraid of thunder. But I don't believe her.

"What's today's date?" the Great One asked Charlie. She took the cotton wool out of one of her ears so she could hear.

Charlie checked her watch. "April twenty-eighth," she said. Charlie's watch can tell the time around the world. It tells the date too.

"April twenty-eighth," the Great One said. "I knew it!"

"Knew what?" I said.

"It's Fluzzy's birthday!"

"We don't know when Fluzzy was born," I reminded her.

"But April twenty-eighth is the day we found him," she said. "Exactly one year ago. Charlie was babysitting that night too. And it was pouring down rain just like now." *Bang!* Another clap of thunder. The Great One stuck the cotton wool back in her ear. Then she called, "Uno." I knew she would win. She always wins.

"We should have a party for
Fluzzy," she said.

"Should we make hats?" I asked.

"First cupcakes," the Great One said.
"Then hats." She jumped up from the table.

"Pointy hats or the other kind?" I asked.

"You choose."

"Really . . . I get to choose?" The Great
One hardly ever lets me choose.

Charlie followed the Great One. "I'm not
much of a baker," she said.

"Don't worry," the Great One said. "I
know how to bake cupcakes."

The Great One stood on a step stool at
the kitchen counter and lined up everything
she needed for the cupcakes.

"I only eat white cupcakes," I reminded
her. "With white frosting on top."

"You think I don't know that?" she said.

"I thought maybe you forgot."

"Well, I didn't."

"OK." Then I got an idea. I'd make place mats for the party. I know how to make place mats because we made them at school for restaurant day. So I got some paper and markers. I started making a picture of a dark and stormy night. I put lightning in the sky. Next I drew a small cat. He was lost and scared and wet. "Remember how we heard Fluzzy miaowing outside the kitchen door?" I asked.

"I heard him first," the Great One said. "And I ran to the kitchen door."

"No, you

didn't! *I* ran to the kitchen door."

"You followed me," the Great One said.

"No, you followed me!"

Charlie said, "I think all three of us got there at the same time."

"But I *saw* him first!" the Great One said. "He was so wet and . . ."

". . . he was shaking," I added.

"I hate when you finish my sentences," the Great One said.

"Abigail," Charlie said, "are you paying attention to the recipe?"

"Yes," the Great One said.

The thunder was moving away now, but it was still raining. I made another place mat. This time I drew Mom and Dad when they saw Fluzzy for the first time. Only he wasn't Fluzzy then. He was: The Lost Cat.

One Year Ago

When Mom and Dad got home that night they were really surprised to see a cat slurping milk from a saucer. "What's this?" Mom asked.

"This is Fluffy!" the Great One said.

"No, it's Fuzzy!" I said. "We saved him from the storm."

"But who does he belong to?" Mom asked.

"He belongs to us now," the Great One sang.

We begged Mom and Dad to let us keep him.

But Mom said, "First we'll have to find out if his owner is looking for him."

And Dad said, "In the morning we'll call the animal shelter."

"And we'll put an ad in the paper," Mom added.

"Why?" the Great One asked.

"Because that's the right thing to do," Dad said. "If you lost your pet, you'd want the person who found him to return him to you, wouldn't you?"

"I'd never let my pet get lost," she said.

We made him a bed with some old towels. He curled up, yawned and closed his eyes.

"Good night, Fluffy," the Great One said.

"Good night, Fuzzy," I said.

The two of us went upstairs to get ready for bed.

"His name is *Fluffy*," the Great One said as we brushed our teeth.

"No, it's *Fuzzy*!" I argued. My mouth was full of toothpaste.

"Fluffy!"

"Fuzzy!"

We both dribbled toothpaste down our chins.

Three days went by. No one knew anything about a lost cat. Not the police. Not the animal shelter. Not the newspaper. Nobody put up a LOST CAT sign with a picture. So we took him to the vet.

The vet told us he was healthy and not even a year old. "What's his name?" she asked.

"Fuzzy," I answered.

"No, it's Fluffy!" the Great One said.

That night Fuzzy was curled up on Mom's lap, purring. She said, "If we're keeping him, it's time to decide on a name."

"I have decided," the Great One said. "It's Fluffy."

"I've decided too," I said. "And it's Fuzzy!"

Dad said, "He needs *one* name. So how

about a combination of Fluffy and Fuzzy?"

"You mean like *Fuffy*?" the Great One said. "No cat wants to be called *Fuffy*!"

"No cat wants to be called *Zuffy* either," I said.

And then all four of us started throwing out combinations.

"Yuzzy?"

"Luffy?"

"Uzzy?"

"Zyuff?

"Fyzu?"

"Fyzu," Dad said. "I kind of like that one."

"Daaad . . ." the Great One said, shaking her head. I shook mine too. No way were we calling our cat *Fyzu*. Instead, the Great One started to say, "It has to be *Fl* . . ."

And I finished with ". . . *uzzy*." We looked at each other and laughed. Then we high-fived to seal the deal.

And that's how Fluzzy got his name.

Unicorn

The Great One

Everything was ready for Fluzzy's party. When the storm ended Fluzzy came back to the kitchen. The Pain said, "Guess what, Fluzz? You're having a party!"

"Don't tell him!" I called. "You'll spoil the surprise."

"You think he knows what *party* means?" the Pain asked.

"Stop . . ." I said. "Before you ruin everything."

"When do we put on his par . . ."
the Pain started to say. Then he
stopped and started again. This
time he spelled it out. "When do we
put his *h-a-t* on him?" he asked.
"Not yet," I said.

When we heard the front door open
Charlie grabbed her backpack and umbrella.
"Wish I could stay for the *you-know-what*,"
she said, "but I have a class at college
tonight."

As Mom and Dad came into the kitchen I
yelled, "Surprise!"

"Are we celebrating something?" Dad
asked Mom. "Did I forget our anniversary?"

Mom laughed. "Our anniversary is in
June."

"Then what?" Dad said.

"We're celebrating Fluzzy's birthday!"
The Pain danced around like he always does

when he's excited. "He came to live with us one year ago. April twenty-eighth. Remember?"

"It was *my* idea," I told Mom and Dad. "*I'm* the one who remembered."

"What a good memory you have, Abigail," Mom said.

"I have a good memory too," the Pain said.

"But not as good as mine," I argued. "I have the best memory in the family. Just ask Grandma. She's always saying so."

"I remember that night," Dad said. "It

was raining even harder than tonight."

I cooed at Fluzzy. "And you were just a lost wet kitty, weren't you?" Fluzzy miaowed. I handed party hats to Mom and Dad. They put them on. I tried to get Fluzzy to wear his too. But he kept shaking it off, then biting it. "Stop that, Fluzzy," I said.

The Pain laughed.

Dad got his camera. After a couple of pictures Mom started sniffing. "Is something in the oven?" she asked.

"Oh no. . . ." I ran for the oven, with Mom right behind me. She grabbed the oven gloves and lifted out the tray of cupcakes.

But it was too late. "They're ruined!" I cried.

Mom tried scraping off the burned part, but nothing helped. What was left of them was hard as wood. "It's all Jake's fault!" I said, then burst into tears.

"My fault?" the Pain said. "What did I do?"

"He kept distracting me." I could hardly get the words out, I was crying so hard. "That's why I forgot to set the timer. And Charlie doesn't even know how to bake! I had to do everything myself."

"Oh, honey . . ." Mom hugged me. "You must be so disappointed."

"I am. I had it all planned. We were supposed to have ice cream with our cupcakes." I caught the Pain watching me. "Stop staring at me!" I told him.

"I'm not staring."

"Yes, you are!"

"Who'd want to stare at you?"

"We can still have ice cream," Dad said. He opened the freezer and lined up the flavours. "What kind for you, Jake?"

"Why bother to ask him when you already know the answer?" I was sniffling now.

"Abigail . . ." Dad began.

"I'll have vanilla," the Pain told Dad. "The white kind, not the yellow. In a dish, not a cone."

"How unusual," I said.

Dad took a deep breath. "Abigail . . ." he said again.

"Oh, that's right," I said. "The little baby can't have a cone because it's not white!"

This time Dad said, "Abigail . . . we're all sorry about the cupcakes. But remember

what we said about being sarcastic?"

Sarcastic is the same as talking *fresh*.
We're not supposed to talk to each other
that way because we're a family. The Pain
is never *fresh* in front of Mom or Dad. When
he feels like dissing me he does it in private.
Then he says *ha ha!* I hate hate hate when
he says *ha ha!*

Dad handed the Pain a dish of ice cream.

"You're making him into such a baby," I
said.

"I'm not a baby!" he shouted.

"Baby is as baby does!" I shouted back.
He hates when I call him a baby.

"Abigail, stop this right now," Dad said.

"Why can't he just eat like everyone
else?" I asked.

"He will when he's ready," Mom said.

"When will that be? When he's twenty-
five? I'll bet he wouldn't have a clue if you

blindfolded him and fed him different foods. I'll bet he wouldn't be able to tell what colour food he was eating then."

"Bet I could!" he said.

"OK . . . let's do an experiment," I said. "My science teacher says we should always be looking for experiments we can do at home."

Dad said, "That would be an interesting experiment, but Jake would have to agree."

"I don't agree," he said. "I'm never going to agree!"

"You spoil him because he's the favourite," I cried. "It's disgusting!"

"Oh, honey . . ." Mom said, hugging me again. "You know that's not true. You know we don't have favourites."

"That's what you say, but I can tell you love him best." I felt myself choking up again.

"Abigail, sweetie . . ." Dad said.

The Pain said, "I don't care if you love *her* best, because Fluzzy loves *me* best. So there!" He picked up Fluzzy and let him lick some of his ice cream.

"Fluzzy loves me as much as he loves you!" I shouted.

"Does not!"

"Does too!"

I tried to take Fluzzy away from him. But Fluzzy jumped down and ran around us in circles.

"Isn't this supposed to be a party for Fluzzy?" Dad asked, handing me a chocolate ice-cream cone.

"She ruined the party!" the Pain said, pointing at me. "Her and her stupid cupcakes!"

"What did you say?"

"I *said* you ruined the party crying over your stupid cupcakes. But who cares, because Fluzzy doesn't need a party to know I love him . . . so *ha ha*!"

That did it! I flew across the room and smushed my ice-cream cone against the Pain's forehead. It stuck there. He looked like a unicorn! The ice cream started dripping down his face. When it got to his mouth he stuck out his tongue and lapped it up. "Um . . . good . . ."

"Did you hear that?" I asked Mom and Dad. "It's chocolate! My unicorn is eating *chocolate* ice cream!"

"I'm not your unicorn. I'm your brother! And I'll always be your brother." He grabbed the ice-cream cone off his forehead, took a look, saw that it *was* chocolate, then kept licking it anyway.

"And I'll always be your sister," I told him. "Your *big* sister. And don't you forget it!"

"How could I forget?"

"You can't. Because if it wasn't for me you'd still be eating *vanilla* ice cream!" Now he wasn't just *tasting* my ice cream, he was gobbling it up as fast as he could. "He's eating my whole ice-cream cone!" I cried.

Mom said, "Don't worry about it." And she made me another one.

After our ice cream we all sang "Happy Birthday" to Fluzzy. And this time when Dad snapped a picture, I think even Fluzzy smiled.

No Hats for Fluzzy

Hats, hats, hats!
Hats for cold white stuff.
Hats for wet stuff.
Hats for riding on wheels.

But no hats for Fluzzy!

She wanted me to wear hats.

That girl with tails coming out of her ears.

I *hissed* to tell her I don't like hats.

But she didn't get it.

She called me *Mister*.

What kind of name is that?

That boy was even worse.
He tried to push me into the bathtub.
Don't you want to learn to swim? he said.
No, I didn't want to learn to swim!
So I *hissed* and I stuck out my claws.
He pulled my tail.
I tried to bite him before he bit me.

They chased me through the house.
Stupid cat! she called.
When the door opened I flew out.
I ran as fast as I could
And as far as I could.
I was never going to let them find me.

When the big booms came I was scared.
But I kept going.
When the sky lit up I shook all over.
But I kept going.
When the water fell from the sky
    I got wet.
But I still kept going.

I kept going until
I was too tired to run any more.
I cried, *Miaow . . . miaow . . .*

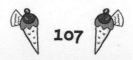

A door opened.

I ran inside.

A different boy and girl lived here.

Ohhh . . . he's so wet, she said.

And he's shaking, he said.

Poor little kitty!

They dried me.
They gave me milk
And a soft place to sleep.

When the mom asked,
But who does he belong to?
I didn't tell.
Besides, I never really belonged to those
    other two,
Even if *they* didn't know it.

These two were different.
They called me Fluffy.
Or maybe it was Fuzzy.
No, wait . . . it was *Fluzzy*.
Anything was better than *Mister*.

After that I was happy
Until the cold white day
When I saw *them* again.

Two Tails and *Tail Puller*.
I heard *Two Tails* say, *I know that cat!*
That cat looks just like Mister.

When she said that my fur stood up.
My whiskers stuck out.
Tail Puller said, *Mister was a bad cat!*

That did it!
I leaped across the cold white stuff
And crept under the house.
I didn't come out till I was sure they
    were gone.

Tonight when the big booms came again
And the sky lit up
And the water came falling down
I hid in my secret place.
In the closet, right at the back,
On top of the towels.

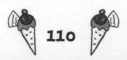

I didn't come out for a long, long time.

When I did *he* said,
Guess what, Fluzz . . . you're having a party!

Party? I tried to remember what *party* means.
It didn't sound good.

She tried to put a hat on me.
I knew *party* wasn't a good word!
No hats for Fluzzy! I told her.

But *she* didn't get it.
So I shook off the hat.
And I bit it a hundred times.

She said, *Stop that, Fluzzy!*
He laughed.
No hats for Fluzzy! I said again.
This time they understood.
They wore hats, but not me.

When they started fighting about who I love
    best
I ran around them in circles.
I love it when they fight over me.

Then I let the two of them stretch me out.
She held my front end.
He held my rear.
I brushed his face with my tail.

They started singing a song.
I think it was about me.
They smiled when the dad snapped our
    picture.
So I smiled too.

I'll stay with them forever.
As long as they remember:
No hats for Fluzzy!

Acknowledgements

With many thanks to Amy Adelson
for sharing her memory of smushing
an ice-cream cone on her brother's forehead.

The Pain and the Great One

Soupy Saturdays

Judy Blume

'Sometimes I think Mum and
Dad love HIM more than me'
The Great One

'Sometimes I think
Mum and Dad love
HER more than me'
The Pain

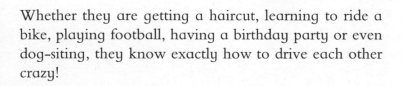

Whether they are getting a haircut, learning to ride a
bike, playing football, having a birthday party or even
dog-siting, they know exactly how to drive each other
crazy!

The Pain *and the* Great One
Cool Zone

Judy Blume

'He never listens to me.
Why doesn't he EVER listen?'
The Great One

'I DO listen.
I just pretend
that I don't'
The Pain

Whether they are telling tales or losing wiggly teeth, little brothers are a real pain. But when the school bully picks on Jake, he can count on his big sister to come running to the rescue!

The Pain and the Great One
Going, Going, Gone!

Judy Blume

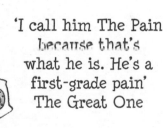

'I call him The Pain
because that's
what he is. He's a
first-grade pain'
The Great One

'I call her The Great One
because she thinks
she's so great'
The Pain

Little brothers are trouble – whether they are sticking
things up their nose, getting lost at the mall or trying to
track down alligators! But are big sisters always right?

A selected list of titles available from Macmillan Children's Books

The prices shown below are correct at the time of going to press. However, Macmillan Publishers reserves the right to show new retail prices on covers, which may differ from those previously advertised.

JUDY BLUME

The Pain and the Great One: Soupy Saturdays	978-0-330-45391-2	£4.99
The Pain and the Great One: Cool Zone	978-0-330-45393-6	£4.99
The Pain and the Great One: Going, Going, Gone!	978-0-230-70028-4	£7.99
Freckle Juice	978-0-330-30829-8	£3.99
Tales of a Fourth Grade Nothing	978-0-330-39817-6	£4.99
Otherwise Known as Sheila the Great	978-0-330-39814-5	£4.99
Superfudge	978-0-330-39816-9	£4.99
Fudge-a-Mania	978-0-330-39813-8	£4.99
Double Fudge	978-0-330-41354-1	£4.99

Audio Editions

The Pain and the Great One: Soupy Saturdays	978-0-230-70663-7	£8.50
The Pain and the Great One: Cool Zone	978-0-230-70836-5	£8.50

All Pan Macmillan titles can be ordered from our website, www.panmacmillan.com, or from your local bookshop and are also available by post from:

Bookpost, PO Box 29, Douglas, Isle of Man IM99 1BQ
Credit cards accepted. For details:
Telephone: 01624 677237
Fax: 01624 670923
Email: bookshop@enterprise.net
www.bookpost.co.uk

Free postage and packing in the United Kingdom